THE GUTLESS GLADIATOR

Snag was better at singing and
dancing than fighting and
bashing people up. Yet the Romans
sent him off to gladiator school,
where all the other gladiators
were big, mean bullies who liked
bashing each other to bits. But Snag
has a trick or two up his toga . . .

MORE BITES TO SINK YOUR TEETH INTO!

LET IT RIP!
Archimede Fusillo
Illustrated by Stephen Michael King

LUKE AND LULU
Bruce Davis
Illustrated by Chantal Stewart

MISS WOLF AND THE PORKERS
Bill Condon
Illustrated by Caroline Magerl

THE GUTLESS GLADIATOR

FIGHTING IS NOT FOR THE FAINT OF HEART!

Margaret Clark
Illustrated by Terry Denton

RUNNING PRESS
KIDS
PHILADELPHIA·LONDON

For my grandson, William. *M.C.*
For Tim. *T.D.*

First published by Penguin Books Australia, 2001

Printed in China

9   8   7   6   5   4   3   2   1
Digit on the right indicates the number of this printing

Library of Congress Control Number: 2005935361

ISBN-13: 978-0-7624-2650-8
ISBN-10: 0-7624-2650-0

Original design by David Altheim and Ruth Grüner, Penguin Design Studio.
Additional design for this edition by Frances J. Soo Ping Chow

Typography: Flyersfont Hardcore, MetaPlus, and New Century School Book

This book may be ordered by mail from the publisher.
Please include $2.50 for postage and handling.
But try your bookstore first!

This edition published by Running Press Kids, an imprint of
Running Press Book Publishers
125 South Twenty-Second Street
Philadelphia, Pennsylvania 19103-4399

Visit us on the web!
www.runningpress.com

Ages 7–10
Grades 2–4

One

Snag was a sad gladiator.

The reason that he was a sad gladiator and not a glad gladiator was that he *didn't want to be a gladiator*!

Some Roman soldiers had come to his village, stolen anything that was valuable, eaten all the food, then burnt down the houses. All the people who were not injured or killed were taken as prisoners, and Snag was one of them.

Now, the emperor of the time was called Titus, and he was really eager to have gladiators so that the crowds could be entertained. He thought it was a great idea to use slaves or prisoners as gladiators because he didn't want his own ordinary everyday people to die for Saturday-afternoon entertainment.

Titus also wanted his own ordinary everyday people to come to the special arena and watch horrible deeds. His empire was a warlike one and he wanted to keep his subjects bloodthirsty, so that when the men had to go to war, they would fight hard and win all the battles. And the women and children would cheer when they came back.

Gladiators were supposed to kill
each other. But if a gladiator was
a brilliant fighter and the crowd liked
him, then the emperor could spare
his life, or, in special circumstances,
even set him free.

The crowd liked gladiators who were good fighters. However, lots of slaves and prisoners didn't have a clue how to fight. So they were sent to gladiator school to learn how to be bloodthirsty.

"I don't want to go to gladiator school," said Snag. "I hate violence. I hate fighting. And I faint at the sight of blood."

"Sorry," said the chief of the gladiators, "you don't have a choice."

Snag frowned. "I'm actually better at singing and dancing and painting than fighting and bashing people up. And I'm really good at telling funny jokes. Would you like me to tell you a funny joke about a Roman candle that went out on a date?"

"No," said the chief of the gladiators. "Here's your packed lunch. Peanut butter sandwiches. And a green apple."

"Smooth or crunchy peanut butter?" asked Snag anxiously. "Brown or white bread? And I like red apples but I could ..."

"Quiet! Stop yabbering and listen. Here's your enrollment card. You're

number ninety-nine. Ninety-nine,
not out. Sounds lucky to me. Have a
nice day."

Snag cheered up slightly. He looked
at his number. Then he frowned.
Was it ninety-nine? Or had the chief
of the gladiators made a mistake?

When Snag held it upside down
it was sixty-six.

For some reason, that didn't look
lucky at all.

Two

Snag's first day at gladiator school wasn't very good.

In fact it was downright terrible.

To start the day, the head trainer told them all to stand in lines. His name was Maximus Taximus, but he was called Maxi Taxi for informal occasions, and Maxi for emergencies, because a gladiator could be dead by the time he said "Maximus Taximus, help!"

"Stand in lions?" squeaked Snag. "In *lions*? What if they eat us?"

"In *lines*, you dimwit," growled
a mean-looking gladiator who looked
like he'd been in gladiator school for
years. But then of course if he'd just
been captured from somewhere he
could be forty and in grade one.

A lot of the gladiators looked old.

Snag figured that they'd been captured because they had been too old to escape.

"How old are you?" he asked a gladiator nearby who was getting ready to line up.

"Eighteen."

"But you look—um—has anyone ever mentioned the words 'sun block with moisturizer' to you at all?"

"Would you like to be wearing your face upside down?" The gladiator glared at Snag as if he was a sausage on a barbecue.

"No."

"Well, mind your own business," said the gladiator over his shoulder as he strolled towards the end of the line.

"*You'll* look like that by the end of the month. It's a very stressful job," said another gladiator.

"Oh. I should have brought some..."

"QUIET!" shouted Maximus Taximus, who now stood out the front. He smiled gruesomely at the students in his gladiator school.

"Good morning, all," he said.

"Gooood moorrrnnning, Maaxximmmusss Taxximusss," the gladiators replied in a slow drawl.

Snag thought this was a very good tactic. If everyone spent the morning drawling they wouldn't have to do any fighting.

"Just call me Maxi otherwise it'll take all day."

Maxi started calling the roll, and obviously each gladiator had to answer. That is, if they weren't dead. Which Snag thought was a strong possibility, as there were only about thirty gladiators and he was number ninety-nine. Or sixty-six. Which meant there were a lot missing.

"Brag the Battleaxe," bellowed Maxi.

"Present, sir," growled this huge gladiator who was standing next to Snag.

Snag froze. Did this mean that each gladiator had to give Maxi a present? He only had his green apple for

a present. He wasn't giving up his
peanut butter sandwiches to *anyone*.

"I didn't hear you," roared Maxi.
"I'll say it again. Brag the Battleaxe."

"PRESENT, SIR."

Snag noted with relief that there
was no present given. Maybe they'd

be handed out later. He looked sideways at Brag the Battleaxe.

Brag had fierce-looking eyes and fists like hams. He looked like he could punch his opponent into the middle of next week.

"Vlad the Vicious," shouted Maxi.

"Present, sir," roared this huge gladiator who was standing on the other side of Snag.

Vlad had one fierce-looking eye and a patch over the other, and fists like legs of lamb. He looked like he could punch his opponent into the middle of next month.

"Slog the Slugger."

"Present, sir," growled this huge

gladiator who was standing behind
Snag. He spat a big slimy glob of spit
that smelt like stale sardines on
a safari in the African jungle. Snag
felt it land on the back of his neck.
Wiping his neck with his sleeve, Snag
stole a quick glance behind him.

Slog the Slugger had piggy little eyes set in folds of greasy flesh and fists like sides of roast beef. He looked like he could punch his opponent into the middle of next year.

Snag glanced around at the other gladiators. They were all really tough. They had cruel faces and muscles like mountains. They looked as if they ate rusty nails for breakfast, barbed wire for lunch, and cannonballs for dinner.

He couldn't see any of the prisoners who had been captured with him from the village. Maybe they'd all been thrown in the sea. Or into the lion pits. Maybe they'd all escaped!

Snag cheered up. Maybe they'd

come and rescue him.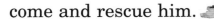

"Now, there's a new gladiator with us today," said Maxi. "Number ninety-nine. Snag the . . . Snag the *what*?"

"Just plain Snag, sir," croaked Snag. "It stands for Sensitive New-Age Guy. I hate violence. I'm more into singing and dancing and painting and telling jokes, really. Did you hear the joke about the goat that turned into a toga? It's a joke about the letters, see. If you . . . "

"Quiet!" thundered Maxi. "You will learn the art of gladiatoring and that's that!"

"But I faint at the sight of blood," quavered Snag. "It turns my stomach."

"You're here to learn to be a
cruel and bloodthirsty gladiator. So
you'd better change your attitude,
boy, or your stomach *will* be turned—
inside out!"

Three

Gladiator school was exhausting.

"You can be a Samnite," Maxi said to Snag. "We need a few more of those because they seem to keep dying off like flies in winter. In other words, they get killed quickly."

"Oh, Mr. Maximus Taximus, I don't think I'd like being a Samnite. Can I be something else?" said Snag anxiously.

"Call me Maxi. And the answer is no!"

"But I . . ."

"Stop arguing. Take this rectangular shield and this short sword. These are the weapons of a Samnite. Oh, and you'd better put this helmet on your head too."

Maxi handed Snag a metal helmet with a visor that could be pushed up out of the way or down for protection. The helmet had a fish engraved on it. The fish didn't look happy. Its mouth was turned down and it looked as if it would love to leap off the helmet and flip-flop across the arena to the sea.

Snag put on his helmet. It was too big and the visor kept slipping down over his eyes and banging him on the nose.

"Um..." said Snag as he tried to peer around his rectangular shield and push up his visor. "I suppose you haven't any see-through shields lying about? Or see-through helmets?"

"Just get on with it," said Maxi impatiently, waving a gladiator who was carrying a net to come over.

"Now, the idea is that this net man will try and tangle you up in his net, then spear you with his trident, okay?"

Snag looked at the net. It looked like the fishing nets they'd used at the village to catch salmon, and it was weighted down at each corner. The net wasn't a problem. But he didn't like the look of the trident. It had three big prongs on the end of a long handle.

"Um . . . " he said. "Could we change over weapons? Like, he can keep the net, I'll give him my short sword and I'll have the rectangular shield and the trident."

"No. We don't change the rules at this gladiator school. Or the weapons.

Just fight Mangler the Entangler and do the best with what you've got," snapped Maxi.

"But I might get hurt." Snag's eyes filled with tears. "And remember, I hate violence. I'm a Sensitive New-Age Guy."

Mangler sneered as he waggled the net. His eyes were cold, like a snake that was ready to strike.

"Don't be such a wimp and a loser," he snarled. "These weapons are only made of wood. We don't use *real* weapons in gladiator school. Now, come on, have a go."

He rushed at Snag with the net in one hand and his trident in the other. Snag held up his shield.

As the net came down, Snag twisted
his short wooden sword into one corner
and spun round and round very fast on
his feet. He couldn't see a thing because
his visor had crashed down again, but
he could hear a lot of grunting.

Finally when he was able to push up
his visor, Snag could immediately see

that Mangler the Entangler was
tangled up. He couldn't prod
Snag through the ropey mass with
his trident. Snag pulled his short
sword out of the tangle and tripped.
His sword got jammed in Mangler's
left nostril.

"Oh. I didn't mean . . ." cried Snag,

and then he went pale, his knees buckled and he collapsed in a heap.

"EeeOW," said Mangler, rubbing the blood with his sleeve as he tried to untangle himself. "You hurt me. That's not fair!"

But Snag didn't hear his protest because he was out cold, flat on his back with his shield over his head.

He'd fainted at the sight of the blood.

Four

Word got around the gladiator school
that the wimpy-looking new gladiator
called Snag had beaten Mangler
the Entangler by tangling him up in
his own net and jamming his sword
up Mangler's left nostril.

This was a gladiator to be
respected and feared, even though
he'd passed out.

Anyone who could get the better of
Mangler the Entangler, one of the best
gladiators in the gladiatorial business,
was a hero.

"It just shows that you can't judge a book by its cover," said Maxi.

"Huh?" said Trevor the Terrible, who hadn't learned to read the cover title let alone a whole book yet, even though he was twenty-four and a half.

"It means that good things come in small packages," explained Maxi.

"Huh?" Trevor frowned.

"It means that sometimes small, weak-looking guys can be terribly, fearsomely lethal." Maxi nodded solemnly.

"But I . . . " Snag began.

"Go and eat your lunch. You'll need to keep up your strength for this afternoon's fight."

This afternoon's fight? Snag gulped.
He'd planned to go to the music room
and play his fife, or go to the art room
and whip up a quick watercolor
painting of some marigolds. Although
come to think of it, he hadn't actually

seen a music room. Or an art room. Or even a school room. The school for gladiators didn't seem to have anything except an arena. And weapons.

"Snag," bellowed Maxi, making everyone jump. "Eat. Or else!"

Snag struggled to unwrap his sandwich. He seemed to be all fingers and thumbs. The way he was going, he'd starve to death. He was a lethal weapon in his own right and he couldn't unwrap his sandwich!

"I hear that you did well against Mangler the Entangler," said Brutus the Beastly, who was sitting next to him. He reached over, flipped

the wrapper off and handed the
sandwich to Snag.

Snag bit into it gratefully. Oh, yuck.
It was creamy peanut butter and
he only liked crunchy. Never mind.
There were more important things
than creamy or crunchy peanut

butter. Like, staying alive.

"How do you think you'd go against *me*? I'm not a net man. I'm a Thracian," said Brutus.

"A Thracian? I thought you were a gladiator."

"A Thracian is a gladiator who

carries a small round shield and
a curved dagger."

"Oh," said Snag. "How do I become
a Thracian? I like the sound of a small
round shield. And I could peel my
apple with the dagger."

Snag bit into his apple and spat out
some of the seeds and the skin.

"You can't be a Thracian. You've been
selected to be a Samnite, so that's
what you are till the day you die."

"So how do I get unselected?"

"You don't. So get used to it," Maxi
interrupted. "Lunch time is over.
Prepare to fight till you drop."

Snag carefully gathered up his
lunchwrap and apple core. He looked

round for a bin but there wasn't one, so he stuffed the garbage down his breastplate next to his fife and, trying not to trip over his short sword or bang his knee with the rectangular shield, he tottered out onto the middle of the arena.

"Go!" bellowed Maxi.

Suddenly Brutus looked like a keen, mean fighting machine. He drew back his lips in a snarl and curled and uncurled his huge hands. Then he flexed his muscles.

"Does this mean the end of our friendship?" called Snag warily.

"Of course not. I'm just getting psyched up."

Brutus waved his wooden dagger
around as if he was trying to slice up
the sky. He held his round shield in
front of him and made some snorting
noises as he rushed towards Snag.

Snag had been given another
short sword but his rectangular shield
was the same. It was heavy to carry.
Puffing slightly, he faced Beastly.
Then, "Wait a minute," Snag called,
"I have to do up my shoe lace."

He bent over just as Brutus

charged at him, swinging the round
shield with one hand and the curved
wooden dagger with the other. He'd
been aiming at an upright Snag, not
one that had suddenly bent over.
Instead of a solid body there was just
a vacant space!

Brutus lost his balance and went flying over the top of Snag, landing in a tangle of arms and legs. His round shield spun like a shiny disk and cut him on the ear. Blood spurted everywhere.

Snag straightened up and turned around.

He saw Brutus lying on the ground in a quivering heap.

He saw the blood.

And he fainted.

Five

"We really have to work on this fainting problem," said Maxi. "You need to build up your strength. Here. Drink this."

Snag looked at the big silver cup that Maxi was holding out. He took it. Then he peered down into the depths of the cup. It looked like thick cocoa. He quite liked a nice hot cup of cocoa before he went to bed. He didn't usually drink hot cocoa in the early afternoon, but rules were rules in gladiator school.

"Do you think you could heat this up?" he asked hopefully. "I do prefer it warmer than this."

"Heat ox blood? We don't usually..."

"Ox blood?"

Snag didn't hear the rest of it because he'd fainted again at

the thought of actually having to drink *blood*.

Slog the Slugger ambled over with a bucket of water and sloshed it all over Snag.

"Glug, glug, glug." Snag sat up, blinking water out of his eyes and spouting it out of his nostrils like a baby beached whale.

"Look," said Maxi. "You're a talented gladiator."

"I am?" Snag's mouth dropped open.

"So far you've only been here a day and you've defeated two of my best gladiators."

"But that was accidental," argued Snag.

"Yes. All right, then, I'll give you a final test. You can fight a net man *and* a Thracian."

"You mean—at the same time?" Snag went white. "That's not fair. Two against one."

"Nothing's fair when you're a gladiator," said Maxi. "Just be thankful I'm not throwing in a couple of chariots with spiked wheels and a tiger or three."

Poor Snag felt desperate. Two against one? Maybe Maxi would choose two small gladiators to even things up a bit.

He didn't.

He chose Thurton the Thrasher,

who was the top net man in the
gladiatorial business, and Sylvester
the Slicer to do the Thracian bit with
his dagger and round shield.

And this time the trident and the
dagger weren't made of wood.

They were made of *real steel*.

Six

Snag knew that this was the end.

No way could he fight Thurton the Thrasher and Sylvester the Slicer and live to tell the tale. No way.

What would happen if he just lay in the middle of the arena on his back with his arms and legs in the air? That's what his dog Ruffia used to do when wild dogs attacked her.

Only one day it hadn't worked. A big black dog had bitten her on the nose.

Well, he could stand it if Thurton and/or Sylvester bit him on the nose.

He just didn't like the idea of being speared full of holes with the trident and hacked up with the dagger.

Snag sighed. It looked like he had to be a Savage New-Age Guy and make the most of it.

"Could I play a final dirge to myself on my fife?" he asked Maxi.

"A final dirge? A FINAL DIRGE? Er, what's a dirge?" bellowed Maxi.

"A sort of final death hymn," said Snag.

"A hymn? We're Romans. We don't believe in hymns." Maxi folded his arms and looked grim.

"You don't? Okay, then can I play a final *her*?" asked Snag.

The other gladiators looked at each
other. This was against the rules.
No one ever requested that he play a
final dirge on a fife. Snag had dragged
out his fife from his breastplate and
was tuning it up. It was a cute little
fife, in fact, more like a whistle,

but the others didn't have the heart
to tell him that.

"Oh, let him play his fife," said
Sylvester. "Then, when I've carved
him up into a million pieces with my
dagger, can I have it?"

"No, *I* want it," argued the

Thrasher. "Once I've poked more holes into him than a sieve, I think the fife should be mine."

"To the victor goes the spoils," said Maxi. "Okay, whoever kills him outright can have it."

"Um—excuse me—but if you kill me then you'll have one less gladiator," explained Snag. "And, if by chance we all get killed, then you'll have *three* less gladiators."

"That's okay, we can get plenty more," said Maxi. "But, just as a favor, just because I'm feeling in a good mood, I'll let you play your whistle."

Snag restrained himself from telling Maxi that he had a real, genuine fife and not a tin whistle. This didn't seem to be a good time to be picky about small things.

"I have another request," said Snag nervously. "Maxi, I think the whole school should have a short break from beating each other up. Instead they

should have a musical experience, don't you think? After all, one's education should be broad and I haven't seen any dancing and art and music yet. Or math. Or science. There seems to be too much physical education at this school, and..."

Maxi smiled. It was more of a gruesome grimace really.

"All right," he said. "We'll have a musical experience. And *then*—we'll have a *killing* experience."

Seven

The gladiators gathered around, leaning on their tridents or rectangular shields, or picking at their fingernails with the points of their daggers.

Together they were a mean, evil-looking bunch.

Snag felt confident. He knew that once they heard his music it would calm them down. It always had this effect. In fact, he'd just finished a small musical recital when his village had been attacked.

Oh, no. If he hadn't played his fife maybe they'd have got riled up and been more aggressive fighting back.

But then again no one could defeat the Roman army, fife or not. The Romans won all the battles and won all the wars. So it wasn't his fault that the village had been burnt and people killed. Not really.

Snag played a few tentative notes.

"That sounds like someone standing on the cat's tail," yelled Brag the Battleaxe.

"I'm just tuning up."

"Get on with it," shouted Maxi. "We haven't got all day. Ten minutes of music and *that's it*."

Snag started to play, a sad mournful
tune that tugged at everyone's heart,
for they all had a heart, and even
though they acted tough and savage,
most of the gladiators were homesick.
Some of them had been captured from
as far away as Africa and hadn't seen

their families for ages. Others had been in jail for doing bad deeds, but they still had families. And memories.

To Snag's horror a lot of the gladiators started to cry and wail.

"Hang on," shouted Maxi at the mob. "*You* can't cry. Gladiators don't *cry*. Not even if they get their arms and legs chopped off. Or their stomachs turned inside out. Or their heads hacked from their necks."

"It's a bit hard to cry if you haven't got a head," Snag said, pausing for breath.

The gladiators wailed even louder.

"Play something to cheer them up," said Maxi, and his voice started to break because he was remembering the first puppy he'd ever had, how it licked his face and retrieved the discus when he threw it. *He* couldn't start crying in front of the whole school.

"Okay, okay," said Snag, because he could feel tears welling up in his own eyes at everyone's distress. "What about a nice eightsome reel or a bit of disco dancing?"

"An eightsome reel? *Disco dancing?*" Maxi stared at Snag as if he couldn't believe his own battered and scarred ears.

"I know the eightsome reel," bellowed Mac the Marauder. "Come on, Glads, I'll teach you. Get into eights."

The next part was rather messy because a lot of the gladiators couldn't count further than five and they kept getting into clumps of seven, nine, and eleven, but finally they were sorted into groups of eight.

It turned out that five other

gladiators knew the eightsome
reel, too, so while Snag played a
lively jig on his fife, the demonstration
group showed the others how to
dance the eightsome reel. (The other
two in the group who didn't know
the eightsome reel got the hang of it

quickly and didn't crash and thump around too much.)

"Okay, everyone. Take your partners for the eightsome reel," roared Mac the Marauder.

Snag started playing. And playing. And playing. The gladiators were having such a fabulous time that they didn't want to stop. They danced on and on until some of them collapsed from weariness. It had become a sort of eightsome-reel *marathon*.

"The one who keeps going the longest is the winner!" yelled Mac the Marauder, because he was sure it would be him.

Soon there were only two dancers

left—Mac and Slog. They thumped and whirled to the faint strains of Snag's fife, and believe me, he was straining. Snag's mouth was sore, his lungs were aching, and right then he didn't care if he never played another tune in his life.

Suddenly a bugle sounded. It made everyone jump. Snag stopped playing his fife as every eye turned towards the great gates. They swung open. In came a golden chariot pulled by two beautiful white horses and surrounded by soldiers riding coal-black horses. The soldiers wore gold cloaks and had gleaming helmets on their head, adorned with plumes of dyed white ostrich feathers.

It was the Emperor's special guard.

And in the chariot was the

Emperor himself!

Eight

"What's going on here?" thundered Titus. "I've come to watch the gladiators training and what have I found instead? A bunch of wimps sitting on the sand, and my two best and fiercest gladiators prancing about arm in arm *dancing*?"

"I can explain," said Maxi. "It's a new— um—it's not what it looks like. It's . . ."

"Excuse me, your Titusship, it's motivational," squeaked Snag. "It's a brand new way of teaching agility, cooperation, and stamina."

"It is?" Titus looked suspicious. "Then why have all these men collapsed in a heap?"

Of course by now the gladiators were standing to attention. They all looked terrified. This was scary stuff. In one thumbs-down motion, Titus could have all their heads collectively sliced from their shoulders by his soldiers.

Vlad was white with fright, Slog had his head down, Brutus was chewing his fingernails, and Brag had a suspicious yellow puddle near his feet.

And Maxi was shaking in his sandals.

"They've been motivationaling for three hours non-stop in the hot sun, your Titusship," said Snag. He felt that it was his fault so he had to try and get the gladiators out of trouble.

"And who are you?"

"This is Snag, the new wonder-gladiator," Maxi interrupted smoothly.

"Him? *He's* the wonder-gladiator? He doesn't look like he's strong enough to pick nose hairs," said Titus.

He climbed down from his chariot and walked around Snag three times, inspecting him carefully.

"He's got no muscle tone, he's got no brute strength, he's got no height or weight or anything of substance,"

Titus said over his shoulder to Maxi. "A string of sausages has got more meat than this lump of useless flesh."

"He's got hidden agendas," said Maxi. He wasn't quite sure what agendas meant but it sounded Roman so therefore it must be good.

"They're hidden all right," scoffed Titus, pinching Snag on the arm. "They're so hidden that they're buried. That's what I think. But we'll find out if we've got a buried treasure here, won't we? I want all of these so-called motivated gladiators in the arena on Saturday. Let's make it a spectacular, shall we? Lions, tigers, elephants, bulls, mad dogs, chariots with spiked

wheels, maniacs with machetes,
the whole caboodle. My people have
started to become bored with mere
fighting. They want action."

He smiled. It was a cold, hard sort
of smile that chilled Snag right down
to his shoe laces. "And I'll especially

be watching this scrawny one." He
jerked his thumb at Snag.

The soldiers sprang to attention.
Had that been an upward jerk? Or a
downward jerk? No, it had been more
of a sideways jerk. Which meant
a maybe.

But on Saturday there'd be no maybes.

It would be a thumbs up from Titus and this scrawny little gladiator could live.

Or a thumbs down.

And that meant death!

Nine

"We've got to practice," said Maxi, looking worried. "Saturday's only two days away. Brutus, start beating up Mangler. Slog, start slamming Vlad. And put some guts into it or you won't have any on Saturday because a chariot spike or an elephant tusk or a bull's horn will have *cleaned you out!*"

"Excuse me, Maxi," said Snag. "I don't think that's going to work."

"Neither do I," sighed Maxi. "There will be ten gladiators milling around at each session and they haven't got a hope."

"What?" shouted Brag. "We haven't got a hope? In that case let's just give up and do some more dancing."

"I think we *have* got a hope," said Snag. "If the arena's chockfull with spiked chariots, elephants, tigers, lions, bulls, dogs, and maniacs, they'll all end up crashing into each other. In fact, they'll probably all end up *killing* each other, which is kind of sad because I quite like elephants, and . . . "

"Face it," groaned Brutus. "We'll be backed into a corner and that's that. No escape."

"We can't be backed into a corner

because the arena's round," said Snag.
"You can't give up!"

"Yeah? Just watch me." Brutus lay
down on the ground with his feet stuck
straight out in front of him and looked
up at the sun.

"Oh, Brutus, you'll get sunstroke
doing that." Harold the Horrible
sighed. "Put your helmet on, there's
a good Glad."

"Why bother? I'm going to die
on Saturday. We're all going to die on
Saturday." And Brutus the Beastly
started to cry.

"Never give up till a blind horse kicks
you in the head," said Snag wisely.
"Gather round, Glads. I have a plan."

It was a bit hard to have a decent circle with thirty gladiators and the head trainer trying to gather around holding their shields, tridents, swords, daggers, and nets, but somehow they did it.

Snag told them his plan.

"That's crazy," said Vlad. "The crowd will get even angrier. They come to see blood everywhere, glorious death in the arena. And you want to give them..."

"Yes, I realize that," said Snag, "but I suspect that they're getting a bit tired of bloodshed and death. There's only so much that a human can take

of that sort of stuff, then people
want something more exciting
and challenging."

"We could use ox blood," said Maxi.
"I've got a vat of it in the coolroom."

Snag went pale.

"No, don't faint. I'm only joking.
But if this plan doesn't get the thumbs

up with the crowd and with Titus, we'll be dead meat for the crows."

Snag looked at the gladiators. He'd grown quite fond of them. Even Slog with his stale sardine breath was sort of appealing in a fishy sort of way.

"Don't worry. The crowd'll love it," he said. "I've heard that they adore mess and mayhem. Plus it's user-friendly and cost-effective, which means that Titus will like it. It will save the Roman government heaps of lira, not to mention gold. Trust me."

Ten

Saturday dawned, bright and clear.

"Visibility's good," said Maxi. "That is, in the sky. In the arena it'll be a dust bowl."

The gladiators were getting ready to pile into the wooden carts that would take them to the arena. They were loading vats of liquid and big blowpipes, slingshots and catapults, soup ladles and all sorts of peculiar items, including special round pots with handles to hook on their belts. The swords, tridents, nets, and daggers were being left behind.

"I hope you know what you're doing," said Mangler to Snag as he gazed forlornly at his net and trident propped against the wall.

"I do," said Snag, who didn't.

The cart they were both riding in jolted and bounced as it was driven through the gate and off down the Appian Way towards the arena.

But what they were about to do was worth a try. Because it was obvious to anyone who had common sense that the gladiators would never survive in the arena against all that opposition. The element of surprise was what they needed, and it was in the big vats.

In a short while they reached the arena. Already the crowd was lining up to get the best seats. They booed and jeered as the wooden carts went past.

"See? No respect," said Slog as a man spat at him.

Slog spat back through the wooden bars and the man nearly threw up when the smelly spit landed on his arm. Served him right.

Finally they were in the special rooms for gladiators. They could hear the tigers snarling and the lions growling. They were probably very hungry and could smell fresh human dinners nearby.

"At least the bulls and elephants and maniacs won't want to eat us," said Snag, trying to cheer everyone up.

"No. They just want to gore us, tread on us, and rip us to bits," replied

Brutus, who was looking scared.

"Okay, Glads," said Maxi. "Come and get your weapons. Pots for everyone. And choose from slingshots, catapults, blowpipes, soup ladles, whatever you want. It's all here."

Soon they were armed and ready.

Trumpets sounded and the people yelled and stamped their feet.

"I've just studied the program. There're some gladiators from other schools first. Then us. Actually our teams are not on till after half time."

"Who goes first?" Harold the Horrible was really nervous.

"Team one."

"Oh. I thought maybe we'd save

the best till last. Team one," said
Harold, who was in team one.

A mighty roar shook the room. The
crowd was thumping and yelling their
heads off. Then there was silence.

"Um, I think that was a thumbs
down," said Maxi.

It was a long and stressful wait
till half time. Someone came round
selling drinks and snacks but no
one was hungry.

Then suddenly a door burst open
and the head gladiator strode in.
He was looking stressed.

"Gladiators are dying like flies out
there," he said. "Swiftly. And swift
deaths mean a bored crowd. So Titus

wants all of you out there together. You
are to fight the animals, the chariots,
the maniacs, and each other all at once."

"What?"

But there was no time to argue.

The trumpet sounded and the huge
doors leading to the arena began to
open.

It was too late to change their minds.

"Charge!" yelled Maxi, and the fight
was on.

Eleven

The gladiators stormed through the
doors, their pots bouncing from their
waists, their weapons in their hands.

"Form the Ring," yelled Maxi.

Dodging the elephants, lions, tigers,
bulls, dogs, maniacs, and chariots
that were spilling onto the arena,
the gladiators formed a double circle,
fifteen in front, fifteen behind, so that
as the first group reloaded, the second
were firing their ammunition.

The crowd was stunned.

Splat. Splat. Splat. Splat.

Great gobs of thick paint went flying through the air.

The lions and tigers didn't like it one bit. They'd spent hours licking themselves and were not pleased to be covered in red, green, yellow, blue, and orange paint.

They skulked off to the edges of the arena to clean their fur. They weren't really hungry anyway because they'd just eaten dead bodies from the first half.

The bulls saw red and charged, but the flying paint confused them, so they turned round and ran the other way, straight into the walls, and knocked themselves out.

The elephants waved their trunks and then decided to get into the spirit of this new game. They dipped their trunks in the vats, which had been dragged out, and started squirting paint at the gladiators, the dogs, and the maniacs.

The dogs and the maniacs were so busy dodging the flying paint that they didn't have time to attack.

"What's going on?" roared Titus.

"Paintball Gladiators. It's the latest craze," yelled Snag above the uproar.

Titus jumped up and turned his

thumbs down. "Kill, kill," he yelled.

"Ah, put a sock in it!" bellowed a big guy in the crowd. "This is fantastic, much better than bloodshed and death. This is *fun*."

The rest of the crowd stamped and cheered. Titus looked worried. He had

his personal army but this crowd was too big. They were shoving their thumbs in the air as they chanted, "Let them live. Let them live."

Titus was no fool. He suddenly realized that this was the answer to the dwindling Gladiator Trust Fund and the ever-increasing protesters who marched outside the Senate waving signs that said, "Kill blood sports."

He held up his hand for silence as the gladiators stood, dripping with paint.

"I declare blood sports and the killing of our noble gladiators to be at an end. I now pronounce that these Paintball Gladiators are the new reigning champions and they will take on the world. Oh, and Rome retains any future television rights."

Snag sagged with relief. His plan had worked.

And from then on, there were no more fights to the death in the arena. The Paintball Gladiators went on tour and raised lots of money for Titus's favorite charity (himself) and other noble charities.

And Snag was officially given a new title: S.N.A.G. Sensitive New-Age Gladiator.

From Margaret Clark

I got the idea for writing S.N.A.G. when I went to see the movie *Gladiator*. I thought, "What if you were a gentle, sensitive new-age guy and you had to be a savage, nasty old-age gladiator?" I logged onto the net to find out about gladiators, and accidently found the ending for my book first!

So if you want ideas for stories, don't forget movies and the Internet can be good sources. And never let anyone bully you!

From Terry Denton

To prepare for this story, I watched 253 different gladiator movies, read 19 books about gladiators, and ate 33 ancient Roman gladiburger meals. My pet nanny goat and I even battled gladiators at the local Roman Ampitheatre. Unfortunately she got eaten by the lion. Do I miss her? No, I'm gladiator!!